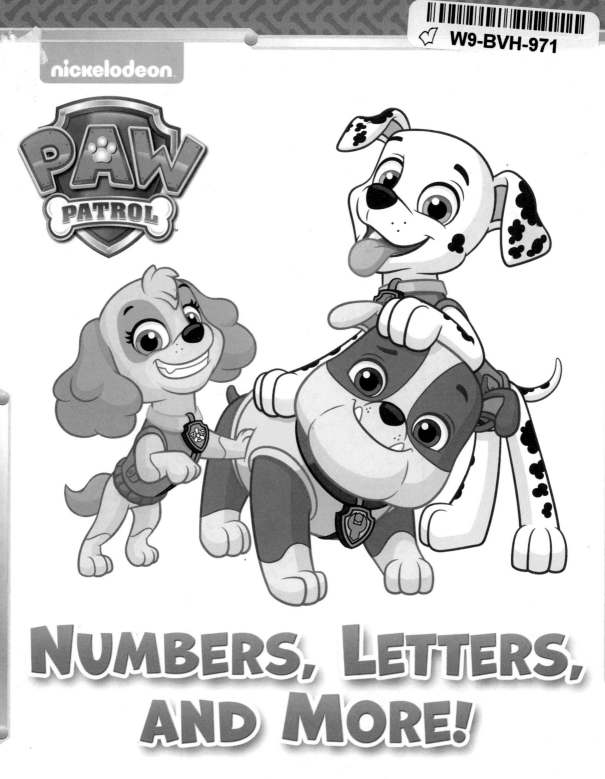

NUMBERS, LETTERS, AND MORE!

A GOLDEN BOOK • NEW YORK

© 2017 Spin Master PAW Productions Inc. All rights reserved. Published in the United States by Golden Books, an imprint of Random House Children's Books, a division of Penguin Random House LLC, 1745 Broadway, New York, NY 10019, and in Canada by Penguin Random House Canada Limited, Toronto. Golden Books, A Golden Book, and the G colophon are registered trademarks of Penguin Random House LLC. PAW Patrol and all related titles, logos, and characters are trademarks of Spin Master Ltd. Nickelodeon and all related titles and logos are trademarks of Viacom International Inc.

ISBN 978-1-5247-6930-7

randomhousekids.com

Printed in the United States of America

10 9 8 7 6 5 4 3

One fearless leader!

Trace the number. Then practice
writing it on your own!

Two brave pups!

Three surprise gifts!

Four bouncing balls!

Five speedy pups!

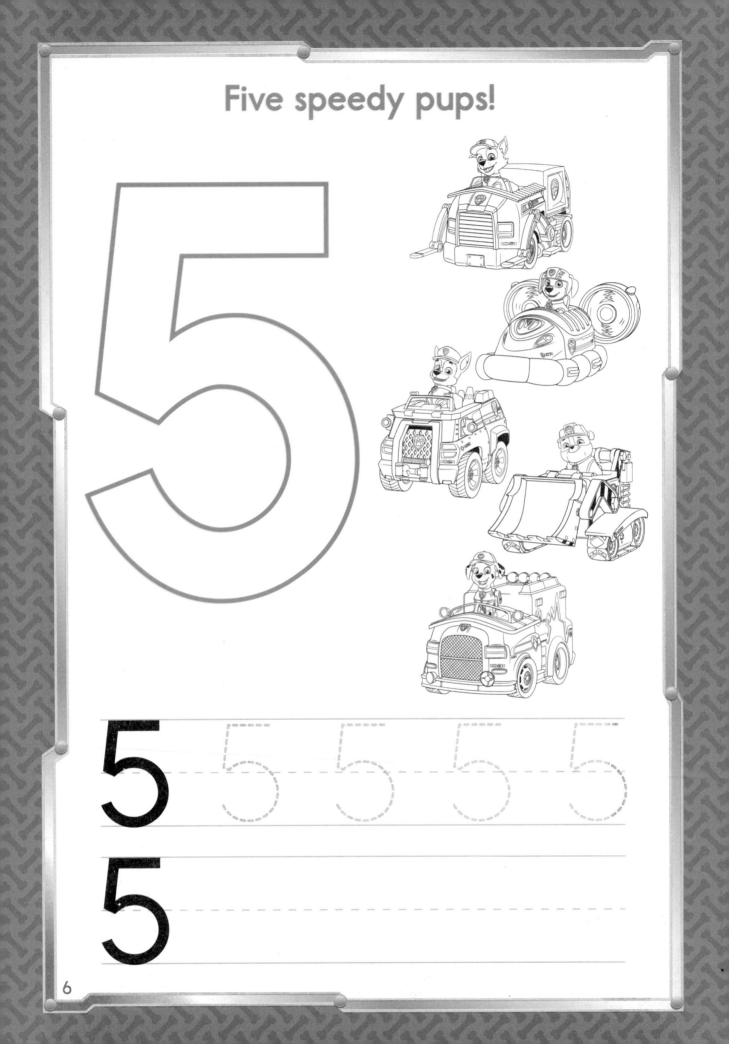

5

Six awesome pups!

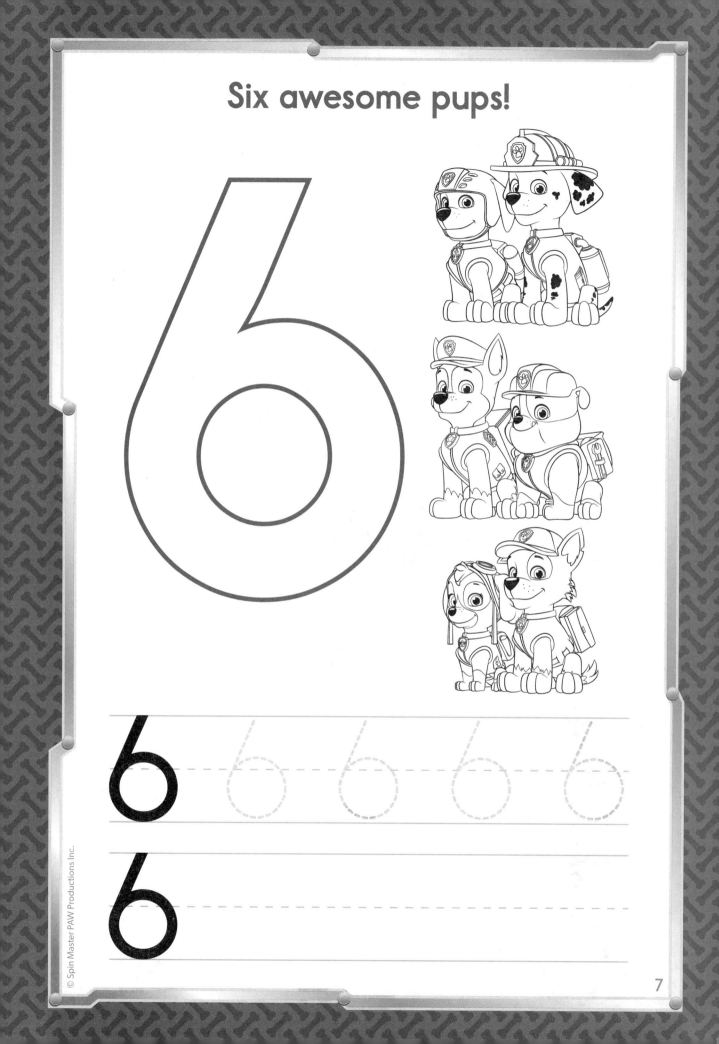

Seven yummy apples!

Eight traffic cones!

Nine flying kites!

Ten terrific treats!

10   10   10   10

10

10

In each section, circle the group that has more.

See answer on page 63.

Color 3 apples red and 5 apples green.

How many pumpkins are there?
Color them orange.

$$+$$

$$=$$

7

See answer on page 63.

Count the pictures in each section.
Write the totals on
the blanks at the end.

See answer on page 63.

Group the pup treats for Skye, Marshall, and Rocky.

Draw a ☐ around the pink treats.
Draw a ◯ around the red treats.
Draw a △ around the green treats.

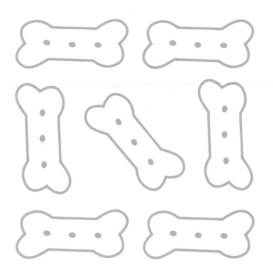

See answer on page 63.

Which path should Chase follow to find Rubble? Choose the one that has the numbers in the correct order from lowest to highest.

Which path should Marshall follow to find Zuma? Choose the one that has the numbers in the correct order from highest to lowest.

See answer on page 63.

Circle the groups that have 3 objects in them.

See answer on page 63.

Count the badges, then draw a line to connect them to the correct number.

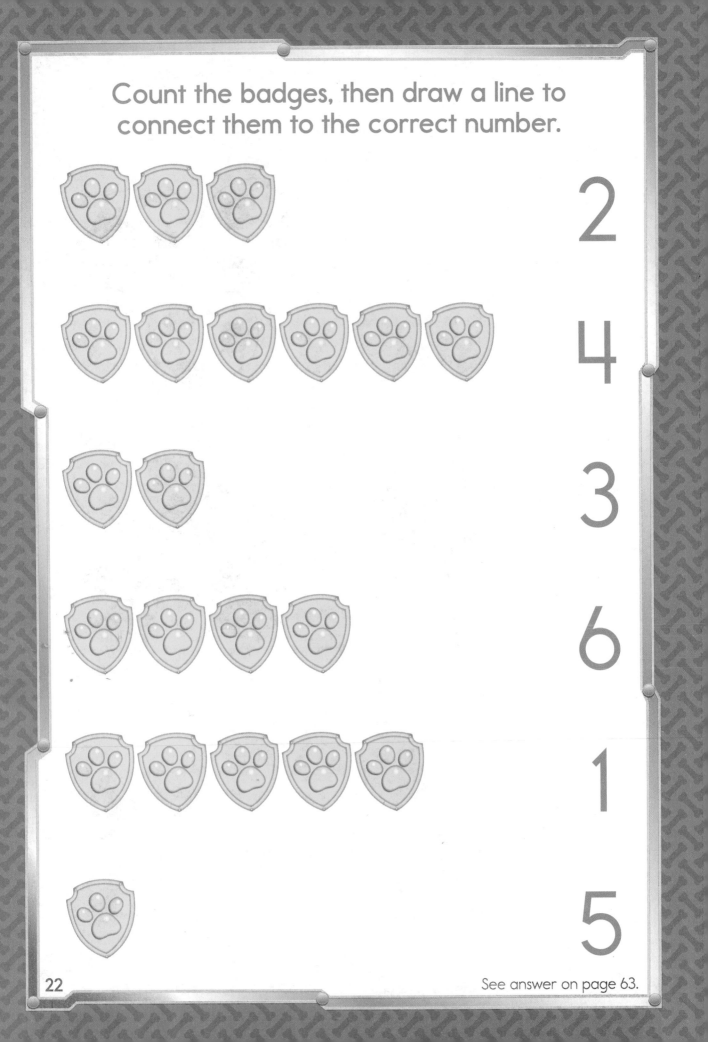

2

4

3

6

1

5

See answer on page 63.

Aa

Color all of
Chase's **apples**.

Trace the letters.
Then practice writing
them on your own!

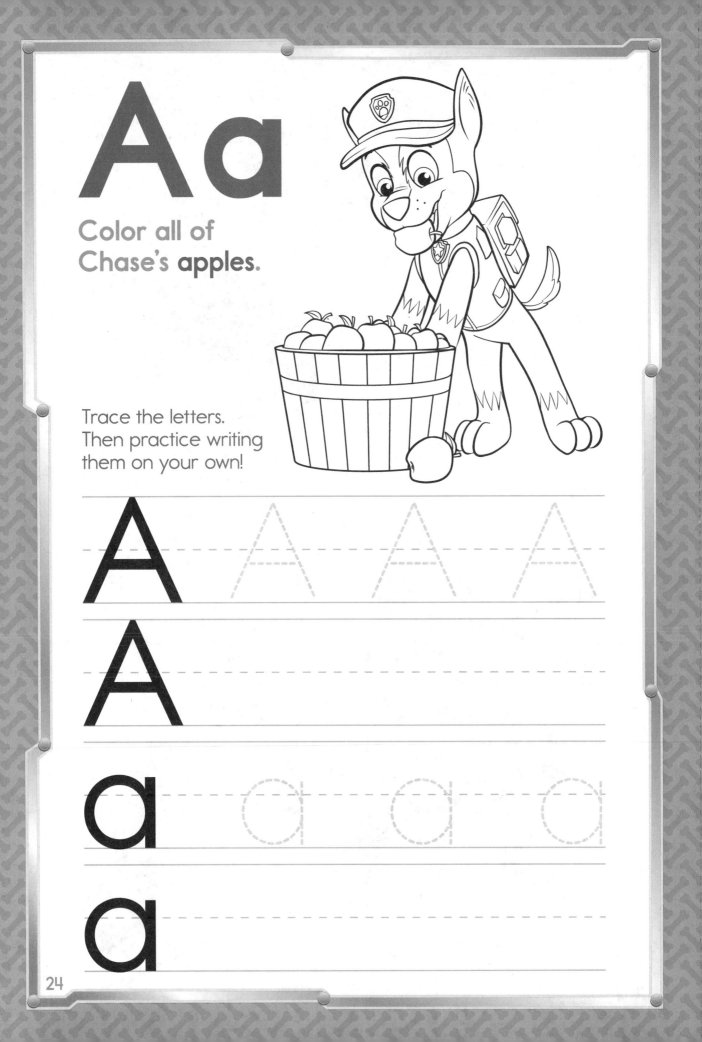

A A A A A A

A A

a a a a a

a a

B b

Color more blue water around the boat.

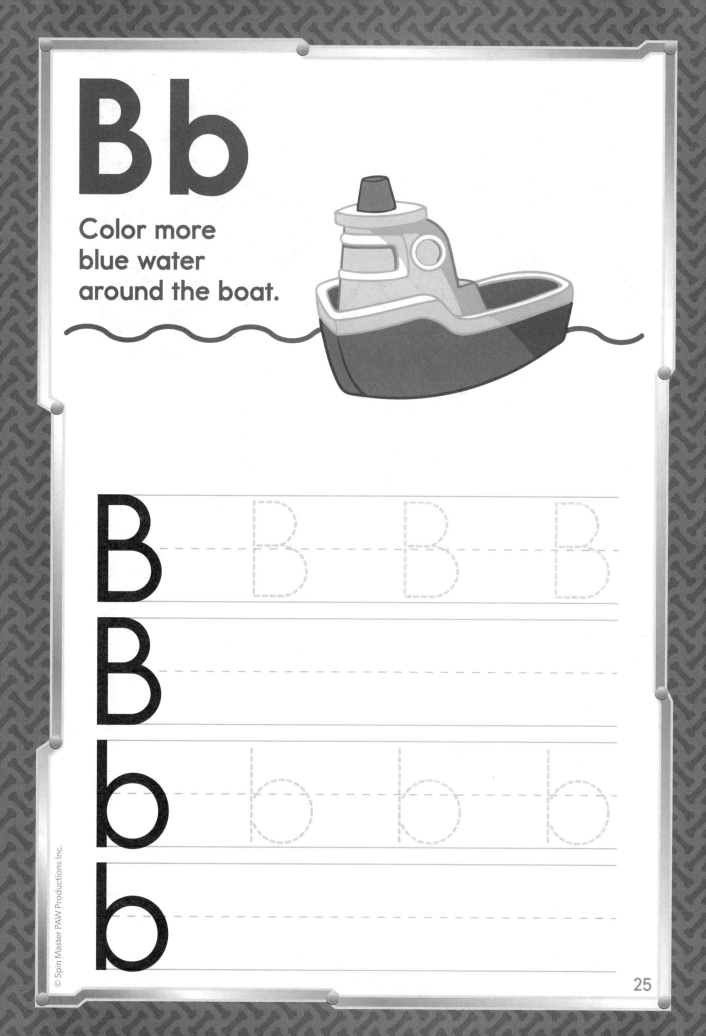

B B B B B

B

b b b b

b

C c

Mr. Porter carries crates of carrots. Color these carrots for him.

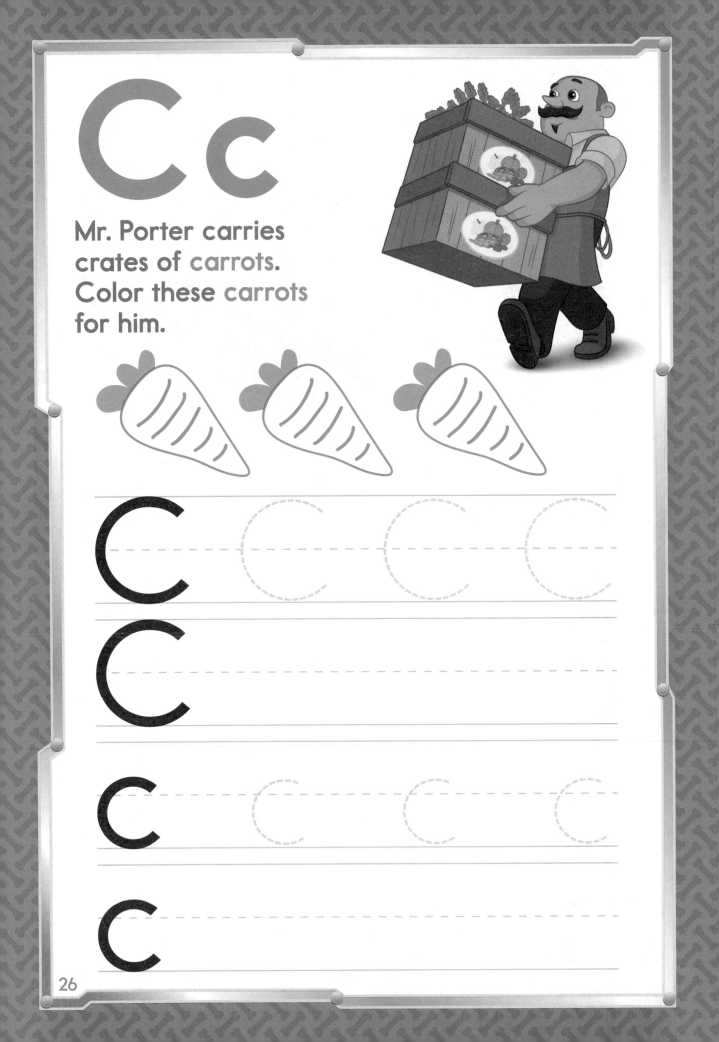

Dd

Good dogs deserve delicious treats!

D D D D D D

D

d d d d

d

Ee

Color these Easter eggs for the pups.

E

E

e

e

Ff

Color the picture
of the farmer.

E E

F F

f f

f f

G g

Ghosts don't scare Chase. Trace the lines to make more ghosts.

G

G

g

g

Hh

Color a helmet and a hard hat for these helpful pups.

Ii

Trace the lines to make some ice cream for Ryder and the pups.

J j

Draw something for Zuma to jump over.

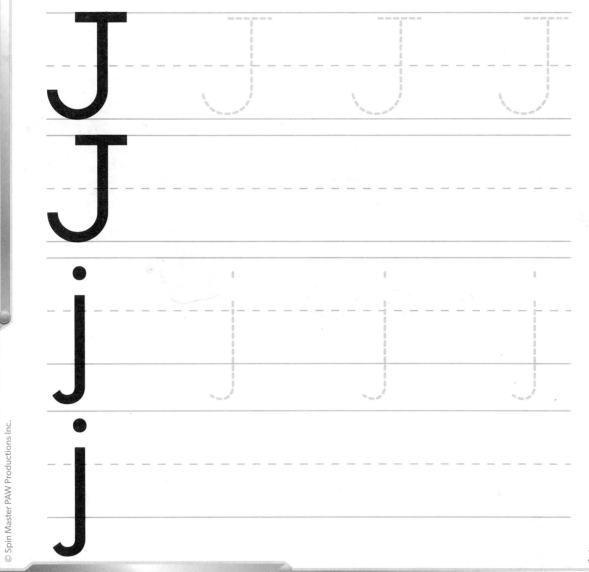

J

J

j

j

Kk

Trace the lines to make a kite for Marshall.

K K K K K

K

K K K K

K

Ll

Rubble is lugging a large log.

Mm

Color Mr. Postman's **mail** for the mayor.

Nn

Chase launches his net. Draw something for him to catch.

N N N N N

n n n n

Cap'n Turbot has an octopus on his head!

P p

Color the pumpkin for the pirate.

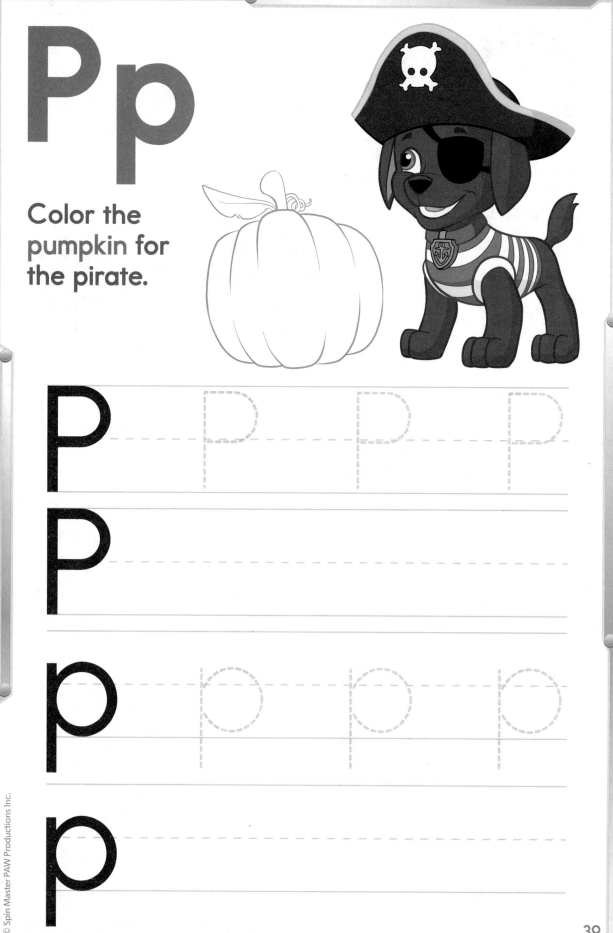

P P P P P

P

p p p p p

p

Qq

Skye wants to be a **queen**. Trace the lines to make a crown for her.

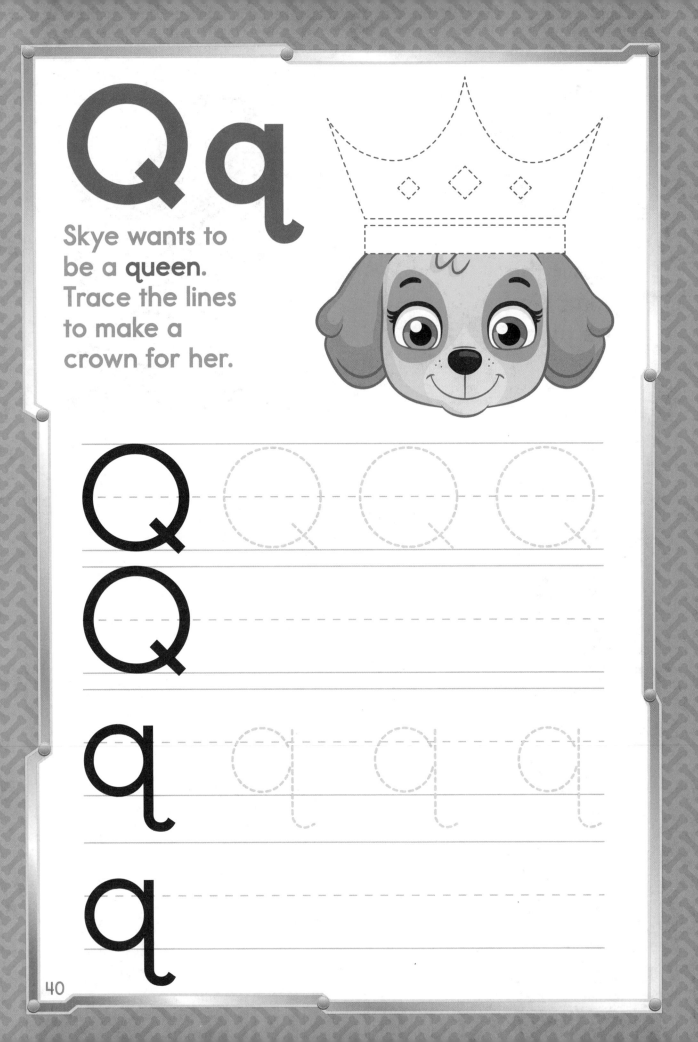

Q

Q

q

q

Rr

Rocky is always ready to reuse and recycle. Put a recycling sticker on his bin.

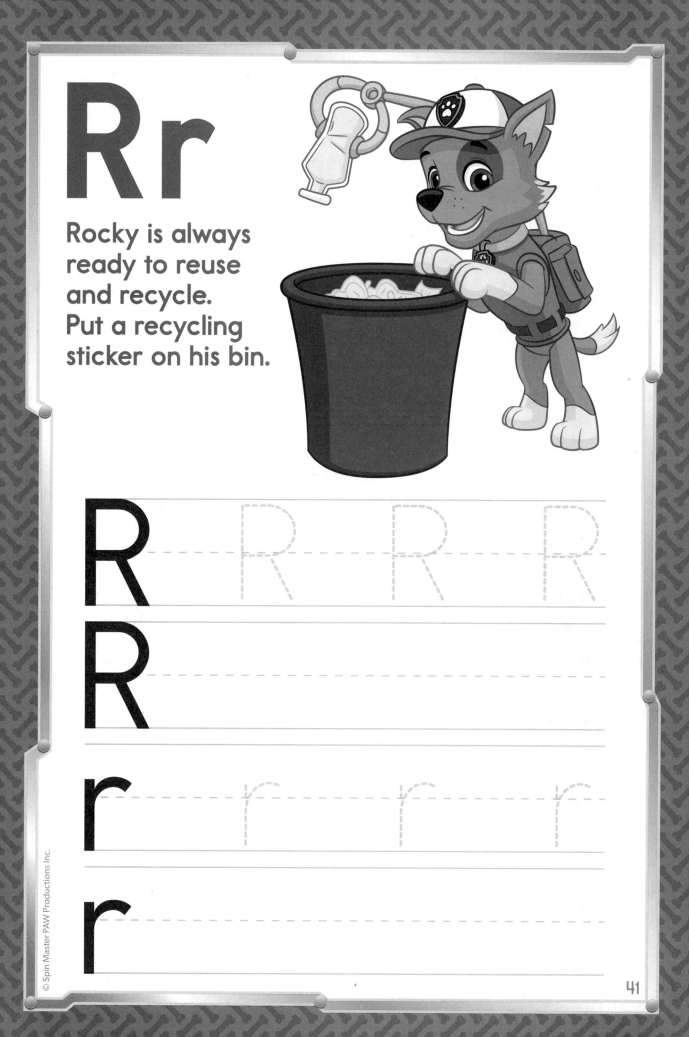

R R R R R R

R

R

r r r r

r

S s

Draw a sun in the sky over the sand castle.

S

S

S

S

T t

Use your stickers to add two more turtles to the scene.

T

T

t

t

Uu

Trace the lines to make an-**umbrella** for Skye.

44

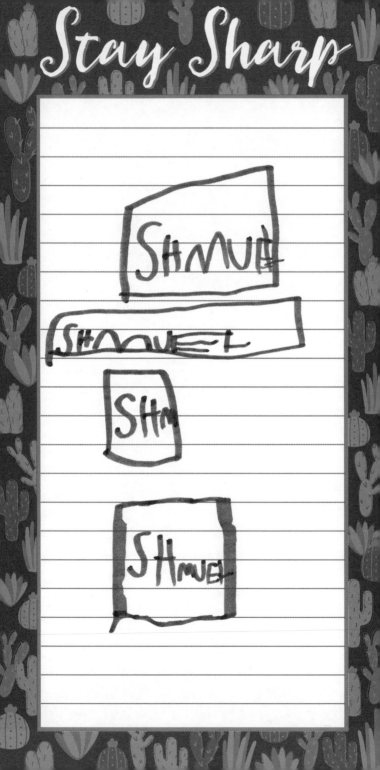

V v

Ryder has a
very cool vest.

45

Ww

Draw some water around Wally the walrus.

W W

W W

W W

W W

X x

Marshall X-rays Cap'n Turbot. Trace the lines to make some extra bones.

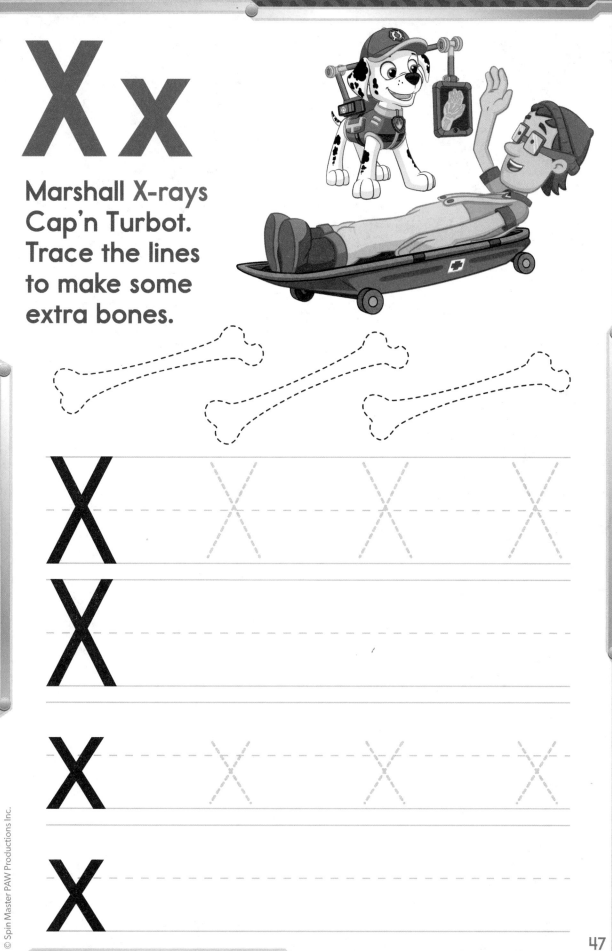

Y y

Color Rubble's
Digger yellow.

Y

Y

y

y

Z z

Connect the dots so Marshall has a zip line to ride down.

Z Z Z Z

Z Z Z Z

Z

Z

Z

Z

D E F G
LMN
RSTU
YZ

Fill in the letters to complete the words.

__ O A T

__ O C K S

__ A T

See answer on page 63.

___ O W L

___ O C K S

___ A T

See answer on page 63.

Chase is setting up cones.
Fill in the missing letters!

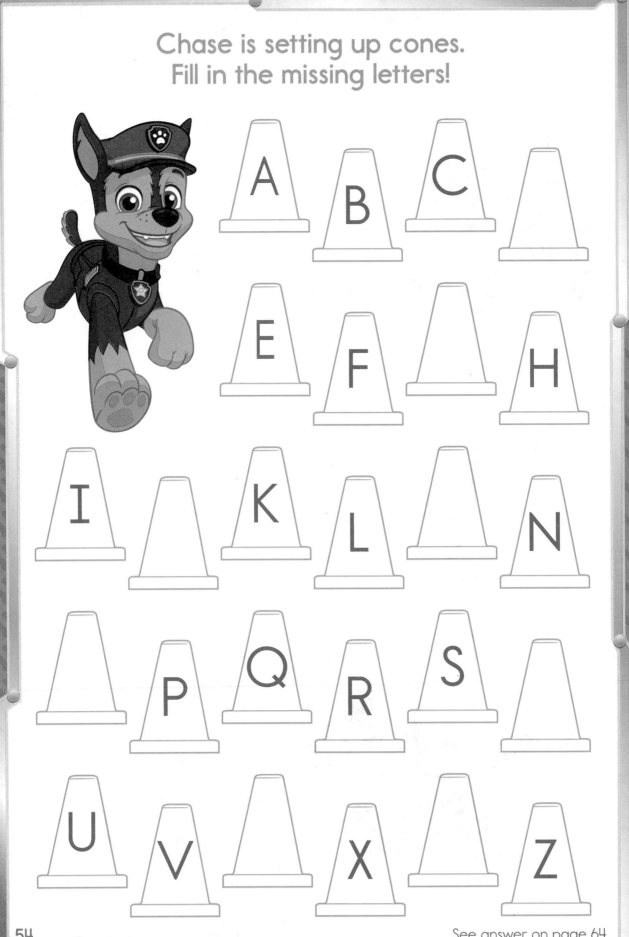

A B C

E F H

I K L N

P Q R S

U V X Z

See answer on page 64.

Help Tracker get to Alex.
Follow the letters from A to Z in the correct order to find the right path.

See answer on page 64.

Write the words.

bird

_____

crown

_____

flower

_____

truck

_____

Each of these words starts with *b*.
Can you fill in the missing letters?

b _ _ _

b _ _ _

b _ _ _

b _ _ _ _ _

b _ _ _ _ _

See answer on page 64.

Some letters are big, or uppercase, and some letters are small, or lowercase. For example, the first letter in your name is uppercase, and the rest are lowercase.

Color all the badges with uppercase letters **BLUE**. Color all the badges with lowercase letters **RED**.

See answer on page 64.

Help the pups find each other.
Fill in the last letter in each column that completes the pattern and the path.

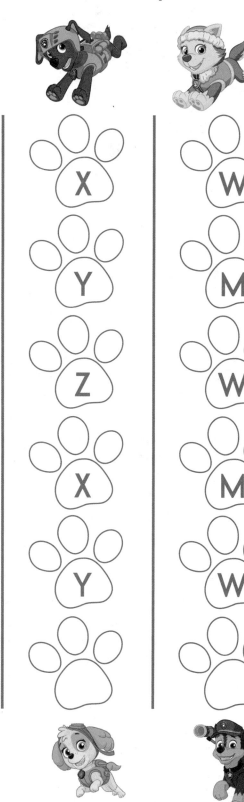

D	M	X	W
E	N	Y	M
F	M	Z	W
D	N	X	M
E	M	Y	W

Help Skye fly to Fuzzy. Follow the path with the letters in the correct order.

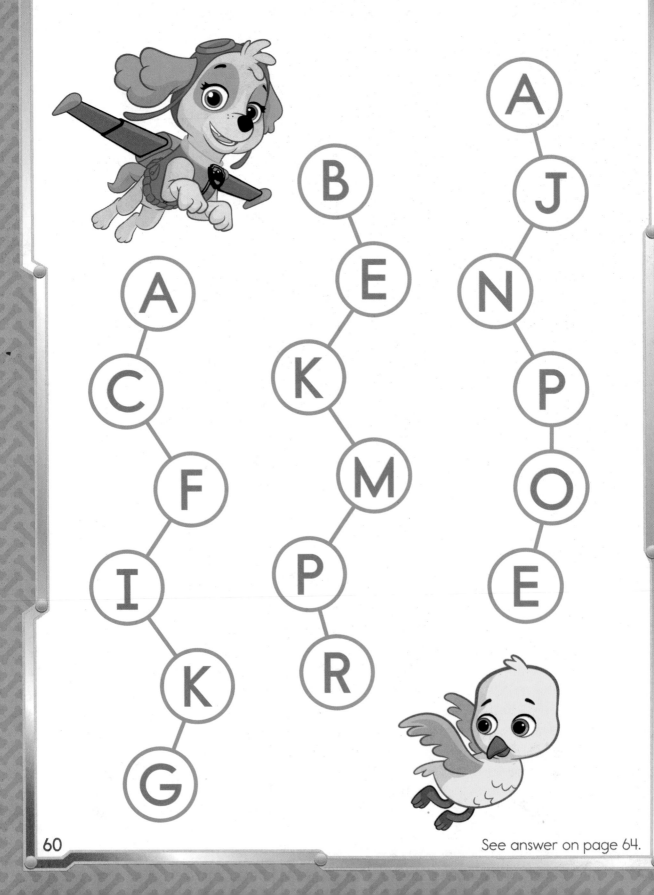

See answer on page 64.

Connect the letters in the correct order to complete the picture.

I KNOW MY LETTERS AND NUMBERS!

Decorate this page with 5 gold stars!

_____

(your name)

Answers

Page 14

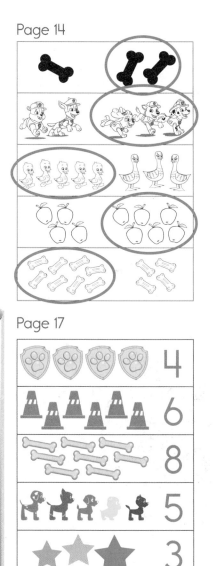

Page 15

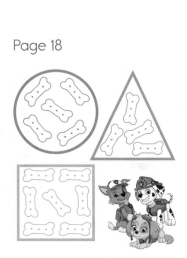

Page 16

$+$

$=$

7

Page 17

4
6
8
5
3

Page 18

Page 19

2
3
5
6
7
8

Page 20

9
7
5
4
2
1

Page 21

Page 22

2
4
3
6
1
5

Pages 52 and 53

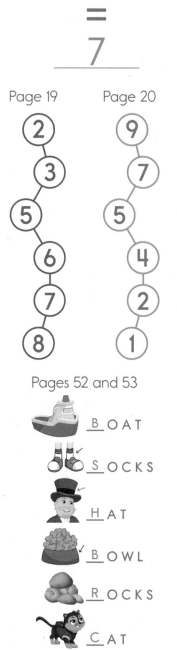

<u>B</u> O A T

<u>S</u> O C K S

<u>H</u> A T

<u>B</u> O W L

<u>R</u> O C K S

<u>C</u> A T

Answers

Page 54

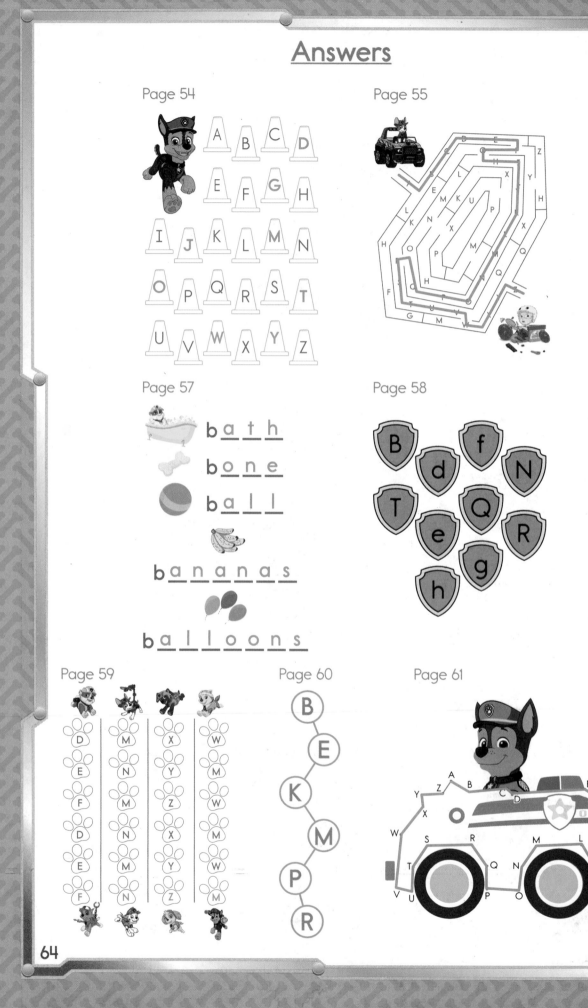

A B C D

E F G H

I J K L M N

O P Q R S T

U V W X Y Z

Page 55

Page 57

b <u>a</u> t h

b <u>o</u> n e

b <u>a</u> l l

b <u>a</u> n <u>a</u> n <u>a</u> s

b <u>a</u> l l <u>o</u> <u>o</u> n s

Page 58

B f
d N
T Q
e R
h g

Page 59

D M X W
E N Y M
F M Z W
D N X M
E M Y W
F N Z M

Page 60

B
E
K
M
P
R

Page 61